DAD JOKES

TERRIBLE JOKES OUR DAD MAKES US REPEAT.

By Andrew and Alice Bardsley

About the Authors:

Andrew and Alice are siblings. Although Andrew and Alice did not write all of these jokes, they have retold them countless times. The illustrations were inspired by Andrew and Alice's original crayon drawings, mostly drawn on napkins at restaurants throughout Tulsa, OK.

Andrew and Alice are Tulsa natives. The children of two eastern Canadian parents, they continue to spend time with their Canadian family at every opportunity.

About the Book:

This joke book was inspired by our dad trying to make us look adults in the eye and talk to them. At first, he would ask us to shake hands and introduce ourselves. Over time, it evolved to introducing ourselves and asking people if they would like to hear a joke. If we delivered our jokes and made eye contact, we were promised a marshmallow. He still owes us a few marshmallows.

Included are a few of our favorites, some we have told, some we have been told. Over many meals we sketched these jokes, asked Book Writing Experts to help us turn the images into this book, and here you are...

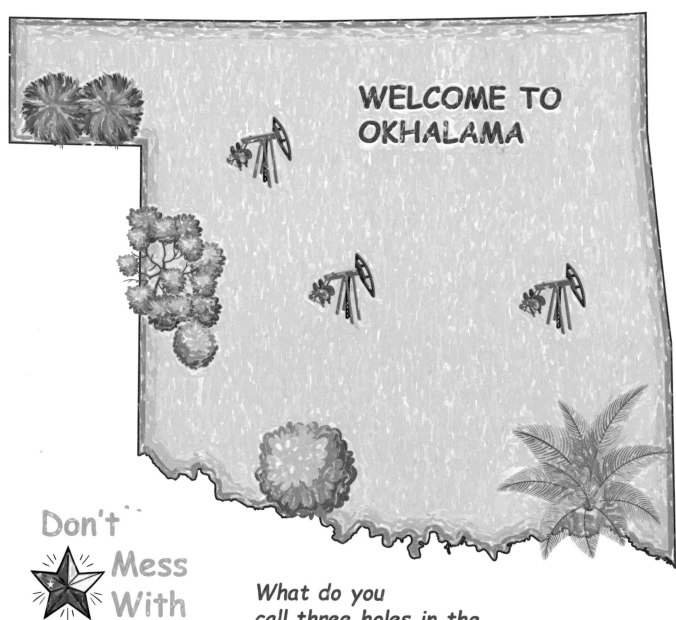

What is a ghosts favorite exercise? A DEADLIFT

How did the Hamburger
Introduce it's Friends?

MEAT
PATTY

WHERE DO SHARKS GO ON VACATION?
TO FINLAND

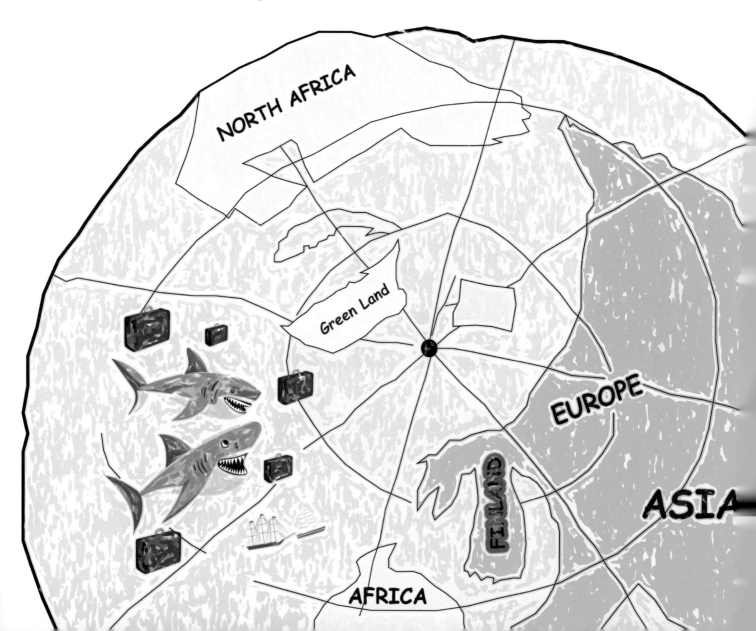

What is a Ballerinas favorite number? Two-Two

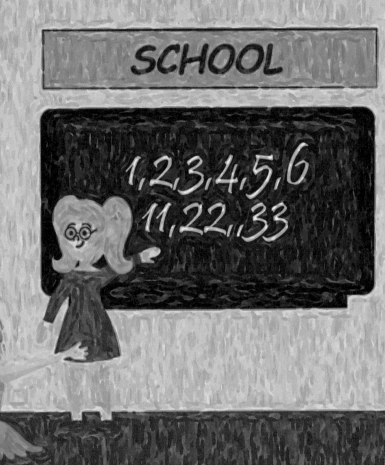

Record your favorite jokes below:

_____

_____

_____

_____

_____

_____

Record your favorite jokes below:

_____

_____

_____

_____

_____

_____

Record your favorite jokes below:

_____

_____

_____

_____

_____

_____

_____

Record your favorite jokes below:

_____

_____

_____

_____

_____

_____

Made in the USA
Columbia, SC
25 November 2024

46695040R00018